Hazelwood Jr. High

by Rob Urbinati

A SAMUEL FRENCH ACTING EDITION

SAMUEL
FRENCH
FOUNDED 1830

NEW YORK HOLLYWOOD LONDON TORONTO

SAMUELFRENCH.COM

MUSIC NOTE

IMPORTANT BILLING AND CREDIT
REQUIREMENTS

HAZELWOOD JR. HIGH was originally produced by The New Group (Scott Elliott, Artistic Director) at I.S. 70 Auditorium in New York City, February 20 – March 21, 1998, under the direction of Scott Elliott with the following cast and production staff:

SHANDA . . . . .Stephanie Gatschet
TONI . . . . Brooke Sunny Moriber
HOPE . . . . Heather Gottlieb
AMANDA . . . . .Amy Whitehouse
MELINDA . . . . Margaret Burkwit
LAURIE . . . . Chloë Sevigny

Set Designer – Derek McLane
Lighting Designers – Brian MacDevitt and James Vermeulen
Costume Designer – Mattie Ullrich
Sound Designer – Kurt Kellenberger
Production Stage Manager – Christine Catti

CHARACTERS

SHANDA – a cute 12 year-old who wants to fit in.

AMANDA – 14, a romantic tomboy.

MELINDA – 15, beautiful, with a swagger that hides her fears.

HOPE – 15, easy going, from a poor family.

TONI – 15, insecure, from a well-to-do family.

LAURIE – 16, troubled, with an evangelist mother.

NOTES ON THE PLAY

HAZELWOOD JR. HIGH is a play about friendship, identity, peer pressure, and sexual exploration. It's about what young teens experience in their "formative" years. It's a play in which a murder happens, but it is not a play about murder.

The focus of the scenes depicting Shanda's murder should focus on the girls' shifting allegiances, and not the brutality. It is important not to show more violence the script indicates. Much of what the girls do should not be seen, as suggested. However, the violence the script indicates is essential.

HAZELWOOD JR.HIGH consists of many short scenes which take place in a variety of locations. The play should move quickly, with no intermission. I've seen various productions which were very simple, using lighting and modular set pieces to suggest locations, four chairs and a steering wheel for the car, etc. The New Group premiere was quite elaborate. Either is fine.

It is important that the beginning of the play does not foreshadow too heavily the later events. Before the murder, the girls were not murderers. In many ways, they are typical junior high school girls with whom the audience can identify. Gradually, the world of the play spins out of control. The early scenes have a lot of humor. The girls are young, and lack a sense of proportion. Sometimes, they say outrageous things to impress the other girls, or to fit in. Often, they lack the words to articulate their feelings. Take care not to "push" for laughs, or comment on the characters.

In the "Statements" and "Psychologists" sections of the play, be aware that the girls are in the criminal justice system. They are not always telling the truth. These sections should be "active," as the girls grapple with guilt and responsibility, construct a defense, or shift the blame.

There are suggestions for types of music throughout the script. All of the songs are by female vocalists of the period. The characters can smoke or not.

Although *HAZELWOOD* considers various issues, it is character-driven, and more psychological than sociological. Hopefully, the play provokes discussion, but it provides no answers.

–Rob Urbinati

"The truth is always audacious"
– August Strindberg

Hazelwood Jr. High is a work of fiction inspired by true events.

Scene One
Shanda's Bedroom

(Music: A song like Tiffany's "I Think We're Alone Now" plays loudly.* Lights up on a small bedroom with clothes strewn about. SHANDA tries on various outfits, checking herself out in a mirror. She writes in her diary [which could be a Voice-Over].)

SHANDA. August 23, 1991. Dear Diary. I can't believe it but it's true. Tomorrow is the first day of school. Let me tell you what I'm looking forward to the most and what I'm dreading the most. Well, this year, I'm goin' to a different school – Hazelwood Jr. High. Thank God! I was so sick of St. Paul's. Now I get to wear cool clothes if my mom lets me. I wish my mom would understand that I don't want to be 12. I want to be 13. I want to talk on the phone on school nights and have people sleep over. I don't know anybody at Hazelwood. I'm sort of scared I won't fit in. I hope they like me. Love, Shanda.

(She adjusts her clothes to look sexier, and dances with abandon. Her confidence builds.)

Scene Two
Lockers at Hazelwood Jr. High

(A school bell rings, and during the announcements, **SHANDA** *heads for her locker.* **TONI**, *wearing big glasses and preppy clothes, and* **HOPE**, *in jeans and a T-shirt, lean against the lockers, chatting. They notice* **SHANDA**.*)*

VOICE-OVER. Announcements for Monday, October 6, 1991. The 4H Club is holding a bake sale in the commons today and tomorrow during lunch period so be sure to try some of their goodies. The decorating committee for the Harvest Homecoming Dance will meet Thursday after school in Room 114. This year's theme is cornucopia. And finally, "Dare to Care" would like to thank everyone who brought non-perishables to the canned food drive last week. It was a big success. Have a great day.

HOPE. *(approaching* **SHANDA***)* Hi.

SHANDA. Hi.

HOPE. You're new here, right?

SHANDA. Yup.

HOPE. I'm Hope. This is Toni-Roni.

TONI. Hi.

SHANDA. Hi. Shanda.

TONI. You don't have a locker partner?

SHANDA. Nope.

HOPE. Lucky.

TONI. Those barrettes are cute. Where'd you get 'em?

SHANDA. They're my cheerleading barrettes from St. Paul's.

TONI. Where's that?

SHANDA. Dixie Highway.

HOPE. You're from Louisville? Cool.

SHANDA. Yeah, but I went Catholic school. I had to wear a uniform.

TONI. I'd kill myself first.

HOPE. You like Hazelwood?

SHANDA. It's OK.

HOPE. It sucks, just wait.

TONI. Only one more year – then high school!

HOPE. Who you been hangin' out with?

SHANDA. No one.

HOPE. Watch out. They don't call it HazelHood for nothin'.

SHANDA. I can take care of myself.

(**HOPE** *notices Nathan offstage.*)

HOPE. *(to* **TONI***)* Look who's here. Get goin', girl.

TONI. I can't! He's with Amanda.

HOPE. You're pathetic. Toni wants to ask you something, Shanda.

TONI. *(to* **SHANDA***)* Would you do me a big favor?

SHANDA. Sure.

TONI. OK, see that guy over there? *(pointing offstage)* With the camouflage pants?

SHANDA. Yeah.

TONI. That's Nathan. We're goin' steady but Hope thinks I should break up with him.

HOPE. He's a dick.

TONI. I can't just walk over there and hand him his ring back.

SHANDA. I'll do it.

HOPE. Alright!

TONI. Thanks!

(**TONI** *takes the ring off and gives it to* **SHANDA***.*)

SHANDA. What should I say?

TONI. Just tell him Toni wants to break up with him.

HOPE. Then kick him in the nuts.

(**SHANDA** *exits.*)

TONI. She's nice.

HOPE. What is she, like, eleven?

(**TONI** *and* **HOPE** *hide near the lockers, listening and laughing as:*)

SHANDA. *(offstage)* Hey, Nathan. Here's your ring. Toni-Roni asked me to give it back to you. Look, she wants to break up with you, OK? Just take it, dickhead!

(**SHANDA** *returns onstage, proudly.*)

TONI. Oh my God, Shanda! I owe you one.

(*Suddenly,* **AMANDA** *bolts onstage and confronts* **SHANDA.**)

HOPE. Hey, girl.

TONI. Hi Amanda.

AMANDA. *(ignoring them, to* **SHANDA***)* What'd you just do?

SHANDA. None of your business.

AMANDA. Yeah well, Nathan's my cousin. You got a problem with him, you got a problem with me too.

(*She pushes* **SHANDA.**)

TONI. *(to* **HOPE***)* Let's go!

HOPE. I'm watchin' this!

(*They move to the side and watch.*)

SHANDA. Look, leave me alone, alright? I was just –

(**AMANDA** *knocks* **SHANDA** *down and sits on top of her.* **SHANDA** *swings at* **AMANDA** *and misses, then pulls her hair.* **AMANDA** *punches* **SHANDA** *in the face. A whistle shrieks.* **TONI** *pulls* **HOPE** *offstage.* **SHANDA** *sits up. She and* **AMANDA** *look into each other's eyes. A bell rings.*)

Scene Three
Detention

(SHANDA and AMANDA in detention, sitting at desks. AMANDA gazes at SHANDA, who's doing her homework. AMANDA opens a notebook and writes. She tears the page out, folds it, makes sure the teacher isn't looking and tosses it to SHANDA. SHANDA, surprised, picks up the note and reads.)

AMANDA. Shana. Hey, so how you like ISS? I think it sucks. If we would'na fought this never woulda happened. Don't think I'm a bad person or nothin'. I hate fightin'. It's just I was gettin' ready to let you have it and I couldn't 'cause you looked so helpless down there. But you pulled my hair so I started hittin'. I want the truth. Do you even know how to fight? If not, don't feel bad. I'll help you, OK? Amanda.

(SHANDA puts the note away and begins writing.)

SHANDA. Dear Amanda. My name's not Shana. It's Shanda – with a "d." It rhymes with yours. You scared me but I don't think you're a bad person if Nathan's your cousin. I don't know how to fight. I didn't fight much at St. Paul's – it was a parochial school. You think I better learn? Why don't you call me sometime? By the way, what does ISS stand for?

(SHANDA folds her note elaborately and tosses it, then puts on lipstick. Music: A song like Debbie Gibson's 'Out of the Blue.' AMANDA reads the note, saves it, and scribbles another note.)

AMANDA. Dear Shanda. Sorry 'bout that! I like that my name rhymes with yours. You think it means somethin'? ISS stands for "in school suspension." You didn't have it at St. Paul's? I got basketball tomorrow but I'll call you maybe Friday or Wednesday. Your friend, Amanda Poo.

(SHANDA and AMANDA smile at each other. A bell rings.)

Scene Four
The Steps Outside Shanda's Apartment Building

SHANDA. Let's sit out here on the steps so I can watch out for my mom. She doesn't like me havin' friends over when she's workin'. 'Specially you because of the fight.

AMANDA. What you tell her?

SHANDA. She's just really strict.

AMANDA. What about your dad?

SHANDA. He lets me do whatever I want. But he lives in Louisville with my step-mom. I wish I could stay with him and have as much fun as possible.

AMANDA. My dad's real strict since my mom moved out but he lets me have girls over anytime I want.

SHANDA. My mom doesn't like me around boys. I had the biggest crush on this guard at Skate World near where I lived and when she found out, she took away my skates. It's cause I'm – I'm only twelve.

AMANDA. Twelve? I thought you were at least thirteen. You look at least thirteen.

SHANDA. Thanks!

AMANDA. You have any boyfriends at St. Paul's?

SHANDA. Lots of 'em. Everyone thought I was boy crazy. I had to sneak around to meet 'em so my mom wouldn't find out.

AMANDA. D'you go all the way with any of 'em?

SHANDA. (*possibly lying*) Uh huh. But I never had a real boy-friend that I loved I don't think.

AMANDA. Shanda, can I tell you somethin'? Promise you won't get mad? Do you know who Melinda is?

SHANDA. Yeah, I love her hair.

AMANDA. Well, um, she and me are goin' together.

SHANDA. (*matter of factly*) How long you guys been goin' out?

AMANDA. 'Bout a year. We met after my basketball game and pretty soon we was hot and heavy. We was seein' each other for 3 or 5 months before she asked me to go steady.

SHANDA. Isn't she like, really popular?

AMANDA. Everyone's just scared of her.

SHANDA. Is she conceited?

AMANDA. She's crazy. My dad kept tellin' me Melinda's a bad person but I didn't listen. She smacks me around just for lookin' at other girls. It's messin' me up.

SHANDA. Amanda, if you're goin' through bad times and you need a friend to talk to, you can always talk to me.

AMANDA. That's so nice. You're so nice. I saw you when you was comin' out for the fire drill today and I thought you looked so nice.

SHANDA. Thanks. I was in Basic Algebra when the alarm went off. I almost fell out of my desk! Then I had Nutrition, then Earth Science, then lunch, then 6th when you saw me, then American Civics.

AMANDA. That's so nice, tellin' me your schedule like that. Shanda, I gotta ask you somethin'. This might sound dumb, but do girls – I mean – do you like girls? I think it's cool cause it's so different. Is that why you're nice to me? Tell me. I won't laugh 'cause I think it's cool.

SHANDA. I don't know, I guess.

Scene Five
The Cafeteria

(**HOPE** and **TONI** enter with lunch trays and sit at a table. **MELINDA** struts in with just a can of Coke. Music: A song like The Bangles' "Walk Like An Egyptian".* She joins **HOPE** and **TONI**, sitting on top of the table.)

MELINDA. Look at Leslie's boobs! They're humungous. They popped right up over the summer. Hey, baby!

TONI. Cut it out, Melinda!

MELINDA. I bet she's got a big bush now, too.

HOPE. (enjoying this) You're whacked out.

(**AMANDA** enters, and sits at the table.)

MELINDA. But not as big as mine, right, Mandy? Little Mandy likes my big bush, don't you, girlfriend?

(She kisses **AMANDA**.)

TONI. What if the monitor sees you!?

MELINDA. (lightly) Suck my dick. (re: something on **HOPE**'s plate) What's that fried thing?

HOPE. Tater Tot casserole.

MELINDA. Gimme some. (eats) Oo look, here comes that new girl. Hey, cutie-pie! (to **TONI**) What's her name?

TONI. Shanda.

HOPE. She's from Louisville.

MELINDA. Hey Shanda. Come and eat at Mel's Place!

AMANDA. Stop yellin'.

HOPE. You guys goin' to Harvest Homecoming? Laurie Tuckett's givin' us a ride.

MELINDA. That chick gives me the creeps. Didn't she sacrifice a cat and drink its blood?

HOPE. No, she only drinks her own blood.

TONI. I'm gonna wear my reindeer sweater.

(**MELINDA** and **HOPE** snicker.)

What – should I wear my cable-knit?

*See Music Note on Page 3

HOPE. Let's go, Toni Roni. Biology. We got frogs today.

TONI. Yuch.

MELINDA. Keep it in your pants, girls.

(**TONI** *and* **HOPE** *exit.* **MELINDA** *notices* **AMANDA,** *distracted.*)

MELINDA. What's the matter, baby?

AMANDA. Nothin'.

MELINDA. Can I come over your house after school? Is your dad workin'?

AMANDA. I don't know. Better not.

MELINDA. *(moving closer)* I miss you, honey.

AMANDA. *(separating)* I got homework.

MELINDA. Please, Poo?

AMANDA. I gotta read.

MELINDA. Read what?

AMANDA. *Anne Frank: The Diary of a Young Girl.*

MELINDA. Just skip to the end part. Look, there's that Shanda. *(shouting offstage)* Hey, little girl! You look tough in those jeans!

AMANDA. You're a perv. Leave her alone.

MELINDA. What's the matter, you like her or somethin'?

AMANDA. You're worse than the guys.

MELINDA. Callin' me a perv. She's still wearin' a training bra.

AMANDA. Shut up!

MELINDA. What's goin' on? *(notices* **AMANDA***'s folder)* What's this? *(picks it up)* Why did you write her name on your folder!? Do you like her? What the fuck is her ugly name doin' on your folder!? You better stay away from her, missy, you hear me? *(throws it down)* I'm gone, man!

(**MELINDA** *exits.* **SHANDA** *enters.* **AMANDA** *hurries to her.*)

AMANDA. Shanda. I'm so sorry, honey. I didn't have nothin' to do with this. If you don't want to see me no more, I understand, OK?

SHANDA. It's OK.

AMANDA. God, I'm really startin' to hate Melinda. I never thought I would but it's happenin'. Next time she talks to me, I'm tellin' her to F off 'cause I'm so pissed. Shanda, listen, OK? I'm all yours, OK?

SHANDA. OK.

AMANDA. Shanda, don't make any plans for Friday. Let's me and you go to the Harvest Homecoming Dance.

SHANDA. What about Melinda?

AMANDA. I wanna be with you.

SHANDA. OK.

AMANDA. Shanda, I have a lot in store for Friday night when we I see you. Know what I mean?

SHANDA. I think, but I can't tell if you're kiddin' or what.

AMANDA. Do you want me to be kiddin'?

Scene Six
Lockers

(A bell rings as **MELINDA** *and* **HOPE** *cross to their lockers and chat.)*

VOICE-OVER. Students, a final reminder. Tomorrow is the last day for you to hand in your picture and your 'You Said It' quote for the 1992 Hazelwood Junior High Yearbook. There are no exceptions. If your picture is not turned in by tomorrow, there will be a blank space in the yearbook where your picture should be. It will look terrible now and for years to come. Get home safely.

*(***TONI*** enters.)*

TONI. What's up?

HOPE. We're gonna kick Shanda's ass.

TONI. I like Shanda.

MELINDA. *(to* **HOPE,** *re:* **TONI***)* Why do you hang around with this one?

*(***SHANDA*** enters.)*

SHANDA. Hi Toni.

*(***TONI*** hurries off.)*

Toni?

MELINDA. Listen up, little girl.

SHANDA. Me?

MELINDA. Yeah, you. Mandy belongs to me. Get your own girlfriend if you like girls.

SHANDA. We're just friends.

MELINDA. You think I'm stupid? I know it was you called Mandy's Tuesday night and hung up when I answered.

SHANDA. I can't talk on the phone on school nights.

MELINDA. Cut the shit. *(pulls out a heart-shaped note)* Did you write this? It stinks of perfume!

SHANDA. *(a beat, then, less convincingly)* That's not my handwriting.

MELINDA. It says, "Shanda loves Amanda?" *(grabbing* **SHANDA***)* Just tell me you two are screwin' 'cause I already know.

SHANDA. No we're not.

MELINDA. Liar! Stay away from Mandy, girlie-girl – I'm warnin' you. *(looks at* **HOPE***)* I have people who can find out. You talk to her again and you're gonna be sorry. Now promise me to my face!

SHANDA. I promise.

MELINDA. Promise what?

SHANDA. I promise I'll stay away from Mandy.

MELINDA. AMANDA!

(She pushes **SHANDA** *against the locker.)*

Her fucking name is Amanda!

(A whistle blows. **HOPE** *and* **TONI** *run off. A bell rings.)*

Scene Seven
Detention

(SHANDA and MELINDA sit at desks. MELINDA writes a note and tosses it at SHANDA, startling her. SHANDA opens the note and reads.)

MELINDA. Shanda. Don't be scared of me, please. I want to be your friend. I just don't like you talkin' to Mandy when I'm not there. You act like you got somethin' goin' on with her. Mandy loves me and I love her so let's just leave it like that, OK? You need to find you a boyfriend because Mandy is mine.

(Bell rings. MELINDA crosses to SHANDA, who is gathering her belongings.)

MELINDA. Hey, girl, how they hangin'?

SHANDA. They're OK. Look, Melinda, nothin's goin' on with me and Amanda, honest.

MELINDA. You, me and Mandy need to have a talk and get this all squared away.

SHANDA. OK.

MELINDA. Where ya headed?

(They walk together.)

SHANDA. King's Daughter.

MELINDA. What's the matter? You sick?

SHANDA. No, I'm a candy-striper. I want to be a nurse.

MELINDA. *(not interested)* Great.

SHANDA. You goin' to the Harvest Homecoming?

MELINDA. Didn't anyone tell you? I hate these dances. Hazelwood can't afford a band and the DJ sucks.

SHANDA. What are you doin' this weekend?

MELINDA. Goin' up to the mall. Last week, me and Crystal got kicked outta there for messin' with the Catholic boys. But I'm goin' back for more – 'cause I'm too slick and I hate dick.

SHANDA. Me too.

(SHANDA smiles and walks away. MELINDA stands still, concerned.)

Scene Eight
Civil War Cemetery Across the Street
from Hazelwood

(Music: A song like Paula Abdul's "Rush" plays in the distance as **AMANDA** *and* **SHANDA** *leave the dance.)*

SHANDA. The decorations were great. The wigs on the pumpkins were so funny. Did you see Toni?

AMANDA. Her and Hope are probably in a car makin' out with some guys.

SHANDA. Where we goin'?

AMANDA. 'Cross the street. No one goes in this cemetery. *(as they walk)* I was walkin' behind you yesterday after Wood Shop and you didn't even know I was followin' you.

SHANDA. *(enjoying this)* Really?

AMANDA. You look sexy tonight.

SHANDA. Thanks.

(**SHANDA** *and* **AMANDA** *sit on the ground.*)

AMANDA. Shanda, do you want what I got in store to happen? Do you wanna make love with me? If you do, just say so. I know it's a big question for such a little girl.

SHANDA. I'm not a little girl.

AMANDA. Shanda, my feelings for you are gettin' stronger and stronger every day. I want you real bad.

(The girls lie on the ground and embrace. They kiss passionately as the lights fade and the music builds. When the lights come up, **SHANDA** *is lying in* **AMANDA**'s *arms. From out of the darkness,* **LAURIE** *enters with a lighter in front of her face. She stares at* **SHANDA** *and* **AMANDA** *for a moment, then wanders off.)*

SHANDA. What was that!?

AMANDA. Laurie Tuckett. Prob'ly lookin' for Hope.

SHANDA. I've never seen her in school.

AMANDA. She quit. She's in therapy or somethin'.

SHANDA. She's scary.

AMANDA. She worships the devil.

SHANDA. You like her bangs?

AMANDA. I like yours better.

> *(They dance closely to the music in the distance.* **HOPE** *enters unnoticed and watches.)*

Scene Nine
Hazelwood Girls Room

(MELINDA brushes her hair as HOPE enters.)

HOPE. Hey, Mel.

MELINDA. Hey, girl. How was the dance? D'ya get lucky?

HOPE. I met this guy and we went to his car but he was drunk and droolin' all over me so I took off. I saw Amanda.

MELINDA. Really? She said she was stayin' home 'cause she had a canker sore.

HOPE. She was with Shanda. They were dancin' together.

MELINDA. In front of everyone!?

HOPE. In the old cemetery. By themselves. Slow dancin'.

MELINDA. You're shittin' me. Yesterday was my birthday, Hope, and –

HOPE. You didn't tell me. Happy Birthday, girl!

MELINDA. Yeah, right, sweet sixteen. Last year on my birthday Mandy wrote a poem just for me – "My Rose of Love." Now she's too busy messin' with that baby-girl to remember. She's gonna teach her everything she learned from me. Mandy didn't even know how to kiss when we met.

HOPE. Get out.

MELINDA. The first time we made out, it was awful – I thought, shit, this girl can't kiss, I gotta do some practice, teach her. She picked it up pretty quick though.

HOPE. Does she act like a guy – when you have sex, I mean?

MELINDA. No. Sex-wise, I'm basically in control. But we haven't done it in weeks now, Hope. She's breakin' my heart.

HOPE. That Shanda's a snake. You gotta watch out for chicks like that.

MELINDA. Me and Mandy are through. I want my panda ring back.

Scene Ten
The Steps Outside Shanda's Apartment

(Music: A song like Mariah Carey's "Emotions".*)

SHANDA. You smell pretty. What is it?

AMANDA. My dad's cologne.

SHANDA. Mandy, ever since the old cemetery, I can't stop thinkin' about you.

AMANDA. *(taking off the ring, very seriously)* Shanda, will you accept this panda ring if I give it to you? Always and forever?

SHANDA. Yes I will.

AMANDA. *(putting the ring on* **SHANDA**'s *finger)* A panda for Shanda from Amanda. *(They kiss.)* "My Rose of Love is sweet and shy. And I'll prob'ly love her till I die." I wrote that just for you.

SHANDA. This means we're goin' steady, right?

AMANDA. You bet.

SHANDA. I'll never take it off. I love you so much, Mandy.

AMANDA. I love you too honey. I loved when you said I love you today after lunch. *(separating herself)* But Shanda, there's one big question I gotta ask you. How come you want to make love every single time I see you?

SHANDA. Isn't that what people in love do?

AMANDA. Love's not just about S-E-X. If you want to have a real girlfriend, that's a lot, not just what happens in bed. Are you just doin' this 'cause it's somethin' new?

SHANDA. When you make love to me – I've never felt like that before.

AMANDA. That's what Melinda says too. Better not wear that ring to school. If she sees you wearin' it, she'll kill me.

Scene Eleven
Limbo

(Alone with a candle, **LAURIE** *recites her poem. Music: A song like L7's "Shove". *)*

LAURIE. The Forest by L. Tuckett. The forest burns. The children scream. Shadows await, to take souls unseen. Stones that mark death await their calling. Innocence allies with evil, hence falling. The children struggle and then break free, running, half flying with hideous glee. But one girl remains who is crying in fear. As the forest burns on, listen and hear.

*See Music Note on Page 3

Scene Twelve
Cafeteria

(**AMANDA** *frets as* **SHANDA** *enters.*)

AMANDA. What's goin' on? I called you like, three times last night but your mom kept hangin' up.

SHANDA. She found a note I wrote you.

AMANDA. Which one?

SHANDA. It said "I love you and want to make love to you" – stuff like that.

AMANDA. What she say?

SHANDA. We had a talk. She asked me if you touched my body in a way you shouldn't. It was creepy.

AMANDA. What'd you tell her?

SHANDA. I said I wrote it like a girlfriend to a boyfriend just for a joke.

AMANDA. She believe you?

SHANDA. She blames it all on you.

AMANDA. It'll be OK, honey. We can still hang out at school and stuff.

SHANDA. She's makin' me switch schools. I gotta go to "Our Lady of Perpetual Help."

AMANDA. Man!

SHANDA. She already talked to Sister somethin', the principal. I have to wear a uniform again! What am I gonna do, Mandy?

AMANDA. Our Lady's not that far. We can still be together. Always and forever, OK? Promise?

SHANDA. Promise.

AMANDA. D'ya say anything to Toni and Hope?

SHANDA. I told Toni.

AMANDA. So the whole school probably knows by now.

(**TONI** *and* **HOPE** *enter.*)

HOPE. *(rubbing it in)* Hey Shanda, that really sucks about "Our Lady." My cousin goes there – she say it's like a prison. They make y'all wear these ugly uniforms –

TONI. *(to* **HOPE***)* Shut up! *(to* **SHANDA***)* I'm sorry you're switchin' schools, Shanda.

MELINDA. *(enters, gloating)* Hi Shanda

(**SHANDA** *runs off.*)

Bye Shanda! I been in a real excited mood all day, right Hope – actin' real stupid and crackin' everyone up. I feel like jumpin' all over you, Mandy, but I'm a good girl.

HOPE. *(enjoying this)* You're messed up is what you are.

MELINDA. *(putting her arm around* **AMANDA***)* I got you all to myself again, baby.

AMANDA. Get offa me!

(**AMANDA** *runs off.* **MELINDA** *is crushed. A bell rings.*)

Scene Thirteen
Notes

(Limbo. **MELINDA, AMANDA** *and* **SHANDA** *read and write [which could be Voice-Overs].)*

(Music: A song like Amy Grant's "Hopes Set High."*)

MELINDA. Dear Poo. I was in the hall and I went past this class and I saw the most beautiful girl in there. She was holdin' her hair back in a sexy way and doin' some work. Do you know her? I think her name starts with A and has six letters. Hey, we get off Thursday and Friday for Thanksgiving – wanna come over my house if your dad lets you? Love, Mel.

AMANDA. Dear Mel. What's goin' on is I need to figure out some things like how you are without me and me without you. Just give me a little time and we'll talk about this later or call later or somethin'. Well, see you around. Love, Amanda.

SHANDA. *(writing in her diary)* Dear Diary. I've been goin' to "Our Lady" for two weeks now and I hate it. There's some cute guys, but I'm goin' steady with Mandy and that's enought for me. This weekend "Our Lady" is havin' its First Friday service in the gym. We can invite kids from other schools so guess who I asked. Love, Shanda.

*See Music Note on Page 3

Scene Fourteen
Hallway in Our Lady of Perpetual Help School

*(Music plays in the distance. **SHANDA** and **AMANDA** kiss in a dark hallway.)*

SHANDA. You feel so good, Mandy. I miss what we used to do in my room.

AMANDA. You seein' any of these guys?

SHANDA. This one guy Ray calls me a lot.

AMANDA. Your mom lets you talk to him?

SHANDA. Sure, she's real nice to him.

AMANDA. What about girls?

SHANDA. I wanna be with you, Poo. I wear your ring to school every day.

AMANDA. That don't mean you love me.

SHANDA. Yes it does.

AMANDA. You think you do but deep down you prob'ly really don't.

SHANDA. Why are you sayin' that?

*(**MELINDA** enters, unseen by **AMANDA** and **SHANDA**, and listens in.)*

AMANDA. OK, listen. I can't hold nothin' back.

SHANDA. You're still seein' Melinda! You told me you guys were through.

AMANDA. She won't leave me alone!

SHANDA. So!?

AMANDA. What kills me is I really want to be with both of you. I have two beautiful girls who love me and I don't know what to do.

SHANDA. You said you were all mine. I wrote Melinda's name on my folder and put a big X through it!

AMANDA. I can't just stop lovin' her. It could take a while, honey 'cause love takes time. I love you too, but I don't know.

*(**SHANDA** turns away.)*

Shanda, I'm lookin' forward to a good future with you.

(MELINDA storms over, grabs SHANDA, and slaps her in the face.)

MELINDA. This is the same shit all over again! I've had it with the two of you!

(She holds AMANDA's arms behind her back, and pushes her toward SHANDA.)

Tell her you love me!

AMANDA. *(a beat, then, to SHANDA)* I love her.

MELINDA. Say my name!

AMANDA. Melinda. I love Melinda.

MELINDA. Tell her you don't love her.

AMANDA. C'mon, Mel.

MELINDA. Tell her!

AMANDA. *(to SHANDA)* I don't love you.

MELINDA. Now tell her to get lost!

AMANDA. Get outta here.

(SHANDA looks AMANDA in the eye, then exits.)

MELINDA. *(grabs AMANDA by the throat)* If you talk to her again I'm gonna kill you, understand? You people are destroyin' me! I'm tired of this shit. You forgot my birthday, missy! I'm real mad at you. *(starts to cry)* Hug me. Hug me!

(AMANDA hugs her. After a while:)

I'm sorry, baby. I got cramps and I'm in a real bitchy mood.

(AMANDA pulls away and runs after SHANDA. MELINDA slumps to the ground.)

Scene Fifteen
Lockers At Hazelwood Jr. High

*(**TONI** and **HOPE** lean against their lockers as a sullen **MELINDA** enters.)*

HOPE. Hey, Mel. Where you been?

TONI. We thought you quit school.

MELINDA. I'm so pissed at Mandy I can't look at her face.

HOPE. Was she at "Our Lady" like I told you?

MELINDA. The two of 'em were all over each other.

TONI. Right in front of the nuns?

HOPE. D'ya kick their ass?

MELINDA. I totally went off on 'em, Hope. They treat me like I'm scum of the earth.

HOPE. Forget about them. Come with me and Toni tonight. Laurie Tuckett's pickin' us up and we're goin' to the Witches' Castle.

MELINDA. That chick's too weird. Does she really drink her own blood?

HOPE. Yeah, but she has a car.

Scene Sixteen
Laurie's Car

(Music: A song like L7's "Fast and Frightening." **LAURIE** *is driving,* **MELINDA**'s *in the passenger seat, and* **HOPE** *and* **TONI** *are in back.)*

MELINDA. So I told her, I go, "Mandy, it's me or Shanda. You can't have your cake and eat it too." I played sick and didn't go to school and when I went back today she starts winkin' at me and I just ignored her and kept right on steppin'. I am so hurt and pissed at her I wanna kill myself.

LAURIE. Want me get in the other lane and smash into that car comin' at us?

TONI. No! What are all these clothes doin' back here?

LAURIE. *(to* **MELINDA***)* I had a thing for this chick Suzette –

MELINDA. You're into girls?

LAURIE. Whatever.

HOPE. Are you makin' this up? You never told me! Damn, everyone I know is muff-divin'!

TONI. What's that?

LAURIE. Suzette was the coldest person I ever met. She moved here from California. *(shows* **MELINDA** *a picture in her wallet)*

MELINDA. She's freaky.

LAURIE. *(puts the picture away)* After that she shaved her head except the bangs.

MELINDA. So then you did it.

LAURIE. She's how I learned about cuttin' myself too. Once I cut real deep on the top of my hand – you could see the bone. *(showing the scar)* Blood was gooshin' out all over. I thought I was dyin', but Suzette just pulls out her camera and starts takin' pictures. I called her my ice princess. She was bad-ass, but I loved her. All of a sudden one day she moved to Utah. I said fuck it. Now I don't give a fuck about a fucking thing.

MELINDA. I wanna be like that. But I hate Shanda, I can't help it.

Scene Seventeen
The Witches' Castle

(A small stone building in the woods. Inside is a small bench and a candle. **HOPE,** **TONI** *and* **MELINDA** *sit on the ground.* **LAURIE**'s *boombox plays a song like P.J. Harvey's "Happy and Bleeding".* * **LAURIE** *stands with her eyes closed, moving her arms "ritualistically.")*

LAURIE. The three witches who controlled the town of Utica lived here in the Witches' Castle. They're buried in a dungeon deep beneath the earth – right where you're sittin'. All that's left is their bones.

MELINDA. *(to* **HOPE,** *not taking this seriously)* What is she, like, Vogueing?

HOPE. Shhh.

LAURIE. If you listen, you can hear them cry in pain.

*(***LAURIE*** sits on the bench. She writhes her body from the waist up, slowly and strangely.)*

TONI. *(to* **HOPE***)* What's she doin' now?

HOPE. She's gonna channel some dead person.

MELINDA. What's that?

HOPE. Dead people come into her body and she talks like them.

TONI. Can she pick any channel she wants?

MELINDA. *(amused)* This isn't TV, retard.

LAURIE. I hear the voices of dead people caught in the spirit world. They want to speak through me. *(She stops moving and listens carefully.)* Someone is callin' me. Who are you? *(a beat, then)* It's Deanna the Vampire. She's callin' my name. Come to me, she's sayin'. Come to me!

*(***LAURIE*** shakes, then becomes limp. Slowly, she sits up, and her demeanor has changed. NOTE: While* **LAURIE** *is not actually "channeling" Deanna, she uses Deanna to express her own pain.)*

*See Music Note on Page 3

HOPE. Who are you now?

LAURIE. *(speaking like a little girl)* I am Deanna the Vampire. I am the evilest person on earth. I would love to kill somebody and watch them die. I see desolation everywhere. A forest is burnin'. Bloody babies are hangin' from trees. I hate God. I want to be a boy. My heart is beatin' real fast and it hurts!

(LAURIE has a few spasms and collapses, then regains her composure.)

HOPE. *(impressed)* You're twisted! *(to MELINDA and TONI, re: LAURIE's cuts)* See that? It's where she jabbed herself with a safety pin. And this –

MELINDA. Why do you cut yourself?

LAURIE. So I can watch the blood ooze out.

MELINDA. Don't it hurt?

LAURIE. It feels good when it's bleeding. All the tension drains away.

TONI. What if one time you cut too deep?

LAURIE. I die.

TONI. I think it's gross.

(LAURIE springs on TONI and grabs her arm. TONI screams. LAURIE releases her and laughs demonically.)

HOPE. That's her devil laugh!

TONI. Why'd you try to scratch me?

LAURIE. I want to drink your blood.

TONI. No way!

LAURIE. *(pulls out a Swiss Army knife)* How 'bout I cut you a little?

TONI. Get away from me!

HOPE. *(volunteering)* I have a scab on my leg.

LAURIE. That'll work. *(She picks the scab, and puts her mouth on HOPE's cut.)*

(Everyone watches in silence for a few moments as LAURIE sucks HOPE's blood – for TONI and MELINDA's benefit.)

HOPE. It tickles!

TONI. This is makin' me sick. Seriously.

MELINDA. She's just showin' off, Toni.

TONI. I gotta get goin'. I got a book report.

MELINDA. And my butt is freezing.

(The girls prepare to leave.)

TONI. *(to HOPE)* I'm doin' mine on *The Secret Diary of Laura Palmer.*

HOPE. How long is it?

TONI. 184 pages.

HOPE. What's it about?

TONI. That girl from *Twin Peaks*, the blonde? She wrote a book.

MELINDA. Tuckett, ever stab anybody with that knife?

LAURIE. It's too small.

MELINDA. What are you doin' this weekend?

(The girls walk toward LAURIE's car.)

LAURIE. Goin' to Louisville – to a punk show. I know the drummer.

HOPE. The A-1 Skate Park! Alright!

TONI. I hate that kinda music.

HOPE. There's tons of guys, Toni-Roni.

LAURIE. *(to MELINDA)* Wanna come?

MELINDA. Yeah, sure. But Tuckett, do me a favor. Before we go to the show, let's stop by Shanda's house. I wanna teach her a lesson.

(LAURIE looks MELINDA in the eye. MELINDA smiles.)

Scene Eighteen
Melinda's Bedroom

(TONI and HOPE try on MELINDA's clothes. MELINDA fixes her hair. LAURIE lies on the floor, playing with her lighter. Music: A song like Taylor Dayne's "Shelter".)*

TONI. You have so many nice things!

MELINDA. My dad bought me tons of stuff.

TONI. *(re: a pair of shoes)* Hope, look at these – Pine Cones! *(to MELINDA)* If they fit, can I wear 'em?

MELINDA. Wear whatever you want 'cept my leather jacket.

TONI. You look so tough in that! *(She squeezes into the shoes.)*

HOPE. This is like the Land of 1000 Bras!

TONI. *(re: shoes)* They're tight, but I'm wearin' 'em anyway.

HOPE. *(holding up a pair of MELINDA's jeans)* You think these'd look good on me?

MELINDA. *(slyly)* It's hard to pull 'em down.

HOPE. Maybe I'll take my top off, and wear this black bra with just my jacket over it. *(She takes off her top, and puts on the bra and jacket.)*

MELINDA. D'you guys see how much Shanda started copyin' me before she transferred? Wearin' tight clothes and stuff?

TONI. Lotsa girls wear tight things.

MELINDA. I gotta show her who's boss.

HOPE. Like how?

MELINDA. We're gonna go get her and beat the shit out of her.

HOPE. Cool!

TONI. What are you gonna just go over there? You don't even know if she's home.

MELINDA. We'll call first.

TONI. And say what?

MELINDA. Tell her we're gonna pick her up.

TONI. She's afraid of you.

MELINDA. You call. She likes you.

TONI. No way.

MELINDA. You can wear my leather jacket.

TONI. What should I say?

MELINDA. Ask if she wants to come to the show. No, I know – tell her Mandy wants to talk to her.

HOPE. That's good. Her mom hates Amanda.

LAURIE. We can take her to the Witches' Castle.

MELINDA. Tell her Mandy wants to see her real bad and she asked you guys to come get her. OK, dial.

TONI. When are we goin' to the concert?

MELINDA. After. Just dial.

    (*Lights up on* **SHANDA.**)

SHANDA. Hello?

TONI. Hey Shanda.

SHANDA. Toni-Roni!

TONI. How's "Our Lady?"

SHANDA. Don't even ask. I miss you, Toni. How you been? You goin' out with anyone?

TONI. I can't stop thinkin' about Nathan. I wish I never broke up with him.

HOPE. Tell her 'bout Amanda!

TONI. Shanda, Amanda wants to talk to you.

SHANDA. Really? She's with you?

TONI. She told me to tell you.

SHANDA. Where is she?

TONI. (*panicking*) Um, she just really wants to –

HOPE. (*grabbing the phone*) Hey Shanda, listen. Amanda needs to see you. She says it's important.

SHANDA. Hope? Where is she?

HOPE. She's waitin'. She told us to come get you.

SHANDA. Who?

HOPE. Me and Toni – and this chick I know with a car.

SHANDA. (*not convinced*) What's she wearin'?

HOPE. Oh you know – flannel shirt, baggy jeans and a base-ball cap.

SHANDA. Come back around twelve o'clock when my mom's in bed. I'll try and sneak out for awhile. But don't beep, OK? Bye.

MELINDA. What she say?

HOPE. She can't come now –

MELINDA. Shit!

HOPE. – but she said to pick her up later.

MELINDA. What if she's not there when we get there? Or she's sleepin'? I had her right in my hands, Hope, and you blew it. Some friend.

HOPE. Relax, Mel – at midnight, she's all yours.

MELINDA. Why'd you tell her what Mandy was wearin'?

HOPE. She asked me.

MELINDA. *(deeply hurt)* Bitch. I want her dead.

TONI. Are we gonna get goin' or what?

MELINDA. I gotta get somethin' in the kitchen.

　　　*(**MELINDA** exits.)*

TONI. Hope, can I do the bra thing too? I don't want to copy you but it'd look cool with the leather jacket. If it's not OK, just tell me.

HOPE. Make sure you take those glasses off.

TONI. *(**TONI** does the bra thing, and shoves her blouse in her purse.)* My mom and dad would kill me if they saw me doin' this.

LAURIE. They should kill you anyway.

TONI. *(to **HOPE**)* I told them I was sleepin' over Leslie's. I'm not allowed to go to concerts yet – except in the after-noon.

MELINDA. *(enters with a butcher knife)* This is the knife I'm gonna use.

HOPE/LAURIE. Cool.

TONI. What're you gonna do with that?

MELINDA: Duh.

Scene Nineteen
Laurie's Car

(*A few hours later.* LAURIE *is parked near* SHANDA*'s apartment building.* MELINDA *is in the passenger seat,* TONI *and* HOPE *are in back. Music: a song like Debbie Gibson's "Only in my Dreams".*)

LAURIE. It's showtime.

MELINDA. (*to* HOPE *and* TONI) You guys go get her.

HOPE. I can't wait! (*gets out of the car*) C'mon, Toni.

TONI. I'm not goin'.

MELINDA. You promised.

TONI. I said I'd call and I called.

LAURIE. Worm.

HOPE. Who's comin' with me? I'm not doin' this by myself.

LAURIE. Let's go, Hope. (*to* MELINDA) You better hide on the back floor.

MELINDA. Don't scare her, Tuckett. Just be really nice and tell her Mandy's waitin'.

(LAURIE *and* HOPE *exit.* MELINDA *hops in the backseat with* TONI.)

MELINDA. (*takes out the knife*) I can't wait till Shanda sees this.

TONI. It looks like the one in *Friday the 13th.* You really gonna cut her with it?

MELINDA. Nah, it's too dull. I'm just gonna tease her a little.

TONI. D'you think Brandon was cute?

MELINDA. Who's Brandon?

TONI. The kid at the concert. The one I went out to Laurie's car with.

MELINDA. D'ya get laid, Toni-Roni?

TONI. You came bangin' on the window.

MELINDA. You still a virgin? What are you waitin' for – you're in junior high for Christ sake.

*See Music Note on Page 3

TONI. I am not a virgin. I told you Todd Thompson made me let him go all the way.

MELINDA. He's a pig. You're lucky he didn't get you pregnant.

TONI. We only did it for one minute – that's it. The guy has to stay inside the girl nine minutes for her to get pregnant.

MELINDA. Who told you that?

TONI. Leslie. Nine minutes for nine months.

(**LAURIE** *runs onstage.*)

LAURIE. *(to* **MELINDA***)* Get down. They're comin'. *(to* **TONI***)* You. In the front.

TONI. *(gets out of the car)* Can I put on WDJX? I hate those cassettes you play.

LAURIE. *(to* **MELINDA***)* You gotta hide. Get down. *(puts a blanket over* **MELINDA***, who crouches down. To* **TONI***)* Put some of those clothes on top. Shanda'll think it's a big pile of laundry back here.

TONI. It is a big pile of laundry.

(**TONI** *throws some clothes on top of* **MELINDA***.*)

MELINDA. *(from under the blanket)* What are you throwin' on me!?

TONI. What? You're under the cover, I can't –

LAURIE. *(interrupting)* Shut up, Toni, here they come. Get in front.

(**HOPE** *enters with* **SHANDA***, whose hair and outfit look a lot like* **MELINDA***'s.* **TONI** *gets in the front seat.*)

SHANDA. Hi Toni.

TONI. Hi Shanda. Your hair looks great.

SHANDA. Thanks.

LAURIE. *(to* **TONI***)* Let Shanda sit in the middle.

TONI. *(to* **SHANDA***)* Skooch over. (**TONI** *sits near the window.*)

HOPE. *(to* **LAURIE***)* Can I drive?

LAURIE. *(handing her the keys)* Don't kill us.

HOPE. I love gettin' to drive!

SHANDA. *(to* **HOPE***)* You have your Learner's Permit?

HOPE. My brothers taught me. But I don't know how to back up yet.

(**HOPE** *gets in the driver's seat and* **LAURIE** *sits in back. They drive off.*)

SHANDA. So where's Mandy at?

HOPE. She's waitin' for you at the Witches' Castle. Up Utica Pike.

SHANDA. What's the Witches' Castle?

LAURIE. You'll see.

HOPE. So Shanda, d'ya hear that Melinda and Amanda broke up for good?

SHANDA. Really!?

HOPE. Now she's all yours if you want her.

SHANDA. I want her, but she's afraid of Melinda. I hate Melinda's guts.

HOPE. That chick is crazy. You better watch out.

TONI. *(trying to warn* **SHANDA***)* Yeah, don't talk about her anymore, Shanda.

(**TONI** *nervously changes radio stations.*)

SHANDA. My mom won't let me talk to Mandy. That's why I was so glad when you called, Toni. I haven't seen her since right after Christmas. We met in the old cemetery and I said, "Mandy, you gotta forget about Melinda. That's all over. I'm your girlfriend now."

MELINDA. *(jumps up, grabs* **SHANDA** *by the hair and puts the knife to her throat)* Surprise!

SHANDA. Owww!

MELINDA. Shut your mouth! I wanna hear all about you and Mandy and if you lie to me I'm gonna slit your throat.

SHANDA. Cut it out!

(**LAURIE** *watches, fascinated.* **HOPE** *enjoying herself, tries to watch as she drives.* **TONI** *frantically changes stations.*)

TONI. I can't find anything good. I shoulda brought my cassettes.

MELINDA. Are you and Mandy goin' steady?

SHANDA. No.

MELINDA. Don't lie to me. There's my panda ring. Give it to me!

SHANDA. No!

MELINDA. Gimme or I'll push this knife in.

(SHANDA reluctantly slips off the ring.)

Put it on my finger.

(SHANDA does.)

Did you go to the Harvest Homecoming Dance with Amanda?

SHANDA. No.

MELINDA. You're so full of shit. Hope saw you, right Hope?

HOPE. Yup.

MELINDA. So you hate my guts, huh little girl?

SHANDA. I was just sayin' that.

MELINDA. Yeah, right. *(pulls SHANDA's hair harder)*

SHANDA. Ouch! I won't talk to Mandy anymore. I promise. Stop it!

MELINDA. Tell me the truth. D'you have sex with her?

SHANDA. *(a beat, then)* Just that once, OK? Take me home.

MELINDA. You're a big liar for such a little girl. You're gonna be real sorry, Shanda.

TONI. It's Tiffany!

LAURIE. Shut that off!

(TONI does. LAURIE turns on her boombox: a song like Siouxie and the Banshees' "You're Lost, Little Girl,"* continues under the next scene.)

*See Music Note on Page 3

Scene Twenty
The Witches' Castle

(Dark and creepy. **SHANDA** *sits on a small bench.* **MELINDA** *is pointing the knife at her. A candle casts eerie shadows.)*

SHANDA. Leave me alone. C'mon you guys. Where's Mandy?

HOPE. You believed us?

MELINDA. You didn't fix your hair like that when you first got to Hazelwood. You tryin to copy me?

TONI. I like your perm, Shanda.

SHANDA. Thanks, Toni.

MELINDA. Well, my hair's naturally curly.

HOPE. *(to* **SHANDA***)* I wonder how pretty it'd look if we cut it all off.

SHANDA. Not my hair, please! I'll stay away from Mandy, I promise.

HOPE. *(taking* **SHANDA***'s arm)* Look – a Mickey Mouse watch.

TONI. Let me see. When'd you get that?

SHANDA. My dad gave it to me for Christmas. It's Minnie Mouse.

*(***HOPE** *takes the watch off, pushes a button and music plays.)*

HOPE. Oh, I knew this when I was little. *(sings along)* "It's a small world after all – (***MELINDA** *joins in)* It's a small world after all – "

LAURIE. *(interrupting)* The people of Utica tried to burn this castle to destroy the witches. *(puts her lighter near* **SHANDA***'s hair)* That's what's gonna happen to you.

SHANDA. Don't, Laurie, please.

MELINDA. Shut your trap.

SHANDA. My mom'll come lookin' for me pretty soon.

MELINDA. Oo, her mommy. I'm scared.

SHANDA. Please, Melinda, let me go. Hope, will you drive me home?

HOPE. What's the rush?

MELINDA. Yeah, the night is young. Shanda, take off your clothes. I wanna see what all the fuss is about.

(**MELINDA** *hands the knife to* **HOPE,** *who wags it at* **SHANDA. SHANDA** *reluctantly takes off her clothes — except a polka-dot bra and panties.*)

TONI. That's mean! You guys are mean.

MELINDA. You saw me wearin' Pine Cones, right?

SHANDA. No, I got 'em for Christmas.

MELINDA. *(picks up* **SHANDA**'*s shoes)* I'm takin' these.

HOPE. Nice bra. Polka dots. Gimme that!

TONI. Leave her alone, Hope! She learned her lesson, right Shanda?

SHANDA. Yes.

HOPE. Shut up, Toni!

TONI. You shut up. I want to get out of here.

SHANDA. Melinda, I'm really sorry I lied to you.

TONI. OK? C'mon, let's go.

LAURIE. *(to* **TONI***)* I got a frog in my pocket and I'm gonna throw it in your face.

MELINDA. Toni, butt out or we'll cut your hair.

LAURIE. *(threatening* **TONI***)* Hope, give me the knife.

TONI. No!

MELINDA. I'm not through with Shanda yet, Tuckett. I been waitin' a long time for this.

LAURIE. *(pulling* **SHANDA**'*s arms behind her back)* Do it, Mel. Go ahead. Hit her.

SHANDA. Cut it out! Don't! I won't –

(**MELINDA** *punches* **SHANDA** *in the stomach — hard.* **SHANDA** *groans in pain, then falls to the ground. The mood changes. Everything becomes very still.* **HOPE** *backs away and stares off into space.* **LAURIE** *pulls* **MELINDA** *into a corner, and they talk privately.* **TONI** *approaches* **SHANDA.***)*

TONI. I'm sorry, Shanda.

SHANDA. They really gonna kill me, Toni?

TONI. No, that knife isn't even sharp.

(**SHANDA** *whimpers.* **TONI** *hugs her, then hands her the blouse she had put in her purse.*)

TONI. Here, Shanda. Put this on.

(**SHANDA** *puts the blouse on, looks around, then bolts offstage.*)

MELINDA. Get her!

LAURIE. Hope – c'mon!

(**LAURIE** *and* **MELINDA** *run off after* **SHANDA**. **HOPE** *follows reluctantly. From offstage, the sounds of a struggle.*)

SHANDA. *(offstage)* Toni! Help me! Toni please!

TONI. *(sits on the bench, alone, and talks to herself)* I don't want to be here.

(*The offstage struggle continues. After awhile,* **HOPE** *reenters and sits with* **TONI**. *She's still holding the knife.*)

TONI. What were you doin', Hope? Were you helpin' them?

(**HOPE** *doesn't answer. The offstage struggle continues.* **TONI** *and* **HOPE** *sit in silence.* **HOPE** *starts to cry, and* **TONI** *takes her hand. After awhile,* **LAURIE** *and* **MELINDA** *reenter.*)

LAURIE. She's knocked out. *(to* **HOPE***)* Open the trunk.

HOPE. I – I can't.

LAURIE. You gonna drive?

HOPE. No.

LAURIE. Give me the keys.

(**HOPE** *does.*)

HOPE. *(to* **MELINDA***)* Is she dead?

MELINDA. Got me.

TONI. What did you do to her?

LAURIE. *(to* **MELINDA***)* C'mon, Mel. Let's get her in the trunk.

TONI. She won't be able to breathe in there.

MELINDA. Duh?

HOPE. What are we gonna do?

LAURIE. Cruise around awhile 'til she dies.

Scene Twenty-One
The Five Star Gas Station

(Music: A song like Madonna's "Vogue."* They are parked at a gas pump. **MELINDA** *and* **LAURIE** *are in the front seat,* **TONI** *and* **HOPE** *are in the back, scared. A payphone is nearby.)*

LAURIE. Hope, you pump. Toni, you're chippin' in for gas. How much you got?

TONI. *(reaches into her pocket)* A dollar sixty-eight. *(hands it to* **HOPE***)* I'm keepin' a quarter 'cause I gotta call someone.

LAURIE. Who?

TONI. Nathan.

MELINDA. What for?

TONI. I just wanna talk to him.

LAURIE. Make it quick.

*(***HOPE** *and* **TONI** *get out of the car.)*

HOPE. *(whispering)* Toni, should I tell that cashier lady there's a girl in the trunk?

TONI. Don't ask me.

*(***TONI** *goes to the phone and dials as* **HOPE** *pumps gas.)*

TONI. Hey, Nathan. Toni. How you doin'? Nothin', I just felt like talkin'. Nothin' much, just cruisin' around. Went to the concert at the Skate Park. You couldn't hear the words. Nathan, I gotta tell you somethin'. Remember Shanda – she gave you back your ring? *(***TONI** *struggles)* No, nothin', never mind. I can't talk now. I just can't, Nathan. What'd you get for Christmas? I got sweaters and cassettes and Oscar the Grouch. And my Big Granny gave me a baby blanket.

*(***SHANDA** *starts to kick.)*

HOPE. *(whispering to* **MELINDA** *and* **LAURIE***)* She's kickin' around back there.

*See Music Note on Page 3

TONI. *(to* NATHAN, *re: Big Granny)* No, she's still alive.

MELINDA. Let's get out of here, Tuckett.

HOPE. The guy at the other pump is lookin' at me weird!

LAURIE. C'mon, Hope. Pay the lady and get in.

(HOPE *exits, and* LAURIE *yells)*

Toni, hang up – we're takin' off!

TONI. I gotta go, Nathan. OK, see ya. *(She hangs up, and shouts to* LAURIE*)* Wait, I wanna get a Diet Pepsi from the Coke machine.

LAURIE. Get in the car!

*(*TONI *gets in the back seat.)*

LAURIE. What did you talk about?

TONI. Nothin'.

LAURIE. What you tell him?

TONI. Nothin'.

LAURIE. Better not or I'll cut out your tongue and eat it.

(HOPE *returns, and squeezes in the front seat with* MELINDA *and* LAURIE.)

MELINDA. What are you doin'?

HOPE. I'm not sittin' back there near the trunk.

TONI. What are we gonna do now?

LAURIE. There's a logging road near my house. *(to* MELINDA*)* We can do whatever we want there.

SHANDA. Help!

(Everyone is stunned silent. Music: a beat, then LAURIE *turns the boombox up loud to drown out any noise: a song like L7's "Shitlist".*)*

Scene Twenty-Two
Laurie's Bedroom

(Music: a song like Siouxsie and the Banshees' "Raw-head and Bloodybones".* TONI looks offstage [out the window]. MELINDA flips through one of LAURIE's occult books. After awhile:)

HOPE. I'm freakin', Laurie!

LAURIE. Trust me, Hope. I always look out for you, right? Lemme read your rune stones. *(She gets a velvet pouch.)*

HOPE. Where'd you get those?

LAURIE. Electric Ladyland – this spirit shop in Louisville. Pick one.

HOPE. *(pulling one out)* It's got an H on it. Hey, my name starts with H! Is that good?

LAURIE. *(to MELINDA)* Gimme that book. *(consulting the book)* H - H - It says "disruption."

HOPE. That's bad, right?

LAURIE. *(Puts down the book and takes HOPE'S hand.)* "The universe will supply support and guidance."

HOPE. So H is good?

LAURIE. The stones don't lie – if you know how to read 'em. *(standing)* I wanna make sure my mom is sleepin'.

MELINDA. Get some food. D'you have any Fritos?

LAURIE. Just Big Red and Diet Pepsi.

TONI. *(quickly)* Diet Pepsi!

MELINDA. Gimme Big Red. I haven't eaten in like, days.

LAURIE. What do you want, Hope?

HOPE. *(lost in her own thoughts)* No, nothin'.

   (LAURIE exits.)

TONI. Mel, what d'you guys do to Shanda on the logging road?

MELINDA. It was very cool.

HOPE. Is she dead yet?

*See Music Note on Page 3

MELINDA. Prob'ly.

TONI. We should just drop her off somewhere and call her mom.

MELINDA. She'll tell if we let her go now. Y'all relax. Once she dies, we'll get rid of the body and no one'll know nothin'.

HOPE. What if she don't die so easy?

TONI. Get rid of the body how?

(*LAURIE reenters and distributes cups.*)

LAURIE. Here you go, Rice a Roni.

(*LAURIE smiles at* **TONI**, *making her suspicious.* **TONI** *puts her drink down.*)

MELINDA. I'm gettin' bored. Can't we watch TV? What time is it – maybe Gilbert Gottfreid's on.

LAURIE. We don't have a TV. My mom's religion forbids it. No make-up, no jewelry – not even jeans.

TONI. She sounds like a fanatic.

MELINDA. She Fundamental?

LAURIE. Pentacostal. She thinks Satan's livin' inside me. She brought her minister guy over and they tried to exorcise me.

MELINDA. How come she lets you dress all Goth now?

LAURIE. Ever since Deanna the Vampire told her I wanted to kill her I can wear whatever I want.

(*Offstage, a dog barks.*)

HOPE. What's that?

LAURIE. Sparky.

TONI. You have a dog? What kind?

(*They listen closely to the sounds of banging and moaning.*)

MELINDA. Sparky woke Shanda up.

LAURIE. I'll take care of it.

(*as* **LAURIE** *exits:*)

TONI. *(nervously chatting, losing control)* Give him some of those Liver Snaps. Puddle loved those. We had a dog once – one of those hot dogs? He used to pee all over so we named him Puddle. Puddle used to hide in the garage all the time and one day my dad came home from work and didn't see him and ran him over. I was so –

MELINDA. *(interrupting)* Shut up, you're drivin' me nuts.

(The barking and moaning continues, then stops. After a moment, LAURIE reenters.)

LAURIE. Let's get out of here.

MELINDA. We can go cruisin'!

TONI. I'm not gettin' in that car.

LAURIE. C'mon, Hope. Come with us.

HOPE. *(a beat, then)* I wanna stay with Toni.

LAURIE. *(looking HOPE in the eye)* You be real quiet. Take a nap or somethin'. Don't wake up my mom. *(to TONI)* And you – stay away from the phone. *(to MELINDA)* It's just you and me, Mel.

(LAURIE and MELINDA exit.)

TONI. Hope?

HOPE. Yeah?

TONI. Should we call someone?

HOPE. Like who?

TONI. Like the cops.

HOPE. We can't, Toni. We're in too deep.

TONI. What are they gonna do now?

HOPE. I don't know.

TONI. You think they're gonna kill her?

HOPE. I hope so.

TONI. You hope so?!

HOPE. Toni, if she don't die, we're in lots of trouble.

TONI. You want her to die? She's just a little girl, Hope.

HOPE. If she don't die by herself, somebody's gonna have to finish her off.

TONI. Why'd you get me into this?

HOPE. You wanted to come.

TONI. I thought we were just goin' to a concert.

(It's quiet a few moments.)

TONI. Hope, do you think I'm ugly?

HOPE. Well, those glasses make you look like a frog.

*(**TONI** starts to cry.)*

HOPE. No, I didn't mean it like that – I meant you should get new ones.

Scene Twenty-Three
Laurie's Car: Country Cruising

(**LAURIE** *is driving.* **MELINDA** *is wired. It's very dark.
Music: A song like Paula Abdul's "Vibe-ology".**)

MELINDA. I was really hurt and pissed, so I break in Mandy's locker and there's all these notes and shit from Shanda and I'm like, 'What this?" so I –

LAURIE. *(interrupting)* There's a creek under this bridge. Let's throw her in.

MELINDA. She'll float to the top and someone'll find her. Just keep drivin', Tuckett. So anyways, I track Shanda down and I'm like "Listen up, little girl, once and for all. If you don't stay away from Mandy, you're –

SHANDA. *(offstage)* Melinda? Mommy?

LAURIE. She's not dead yet.

MELINDA. Take care of her, Tuckett.

(**LAURIE** *gets out of the car. There are loud thumping
sounds. After a few moments,* **LAURIE** *jumps back in the
front seat.*)

MELINDA. So meanwhile, I find out from Hope that Mandy was goin' over to Shanda's house all the time and –

LAURIE. Shut up about Mandy, will ya?

MELINDA. You love my ass, don't you Tuckett?

(**LAURIE** *plays one of her cassettes, loud. A song like
P.J. Harvey's "Happy and Bleeding."* She puts her arm
around* **MELINDA** *and pulls her closer. They seem con-
tent. After awhile,* **SHANDA** *begins to bang on the trunk.*
LAURIE *turns down the music to listen.*)

MELINDA. This chick is like *The Terminator.* We should pull her out and run her over.

LAURIE. Not with my car we're not.

MELINDA. So what are we just gonna drive around for the rest of our lives?

*See Music Note on Page 3

LAURIE. It's gettin' light out. We gotta do somethin'.

MELINDA. Like what?

(**LAURIE** *clicks her lighter and puts it in front of* **MELIN-DA***'s face. She and* **MELINDA** *stare at it, then look into each other's eyes.*)

Scene Twenty-Four
Lemon Road

(Later that morning. **LAURIE***'s car is parked.* **MELINDA** *and* **LAURIE** *stare into the open trunk, fascinated.* **TONI** *and* **HOPE** *stand apart. NOTE: The audience can't see* **SHANDA**.*)*

TONI. Why d'you come back and get us?

MELINDA. Grow some balls, Toni.

LAURIE. C'mere, Hope.

*(***HOPE*** *crosses to the trunk, and stares in silence.)*

LAURIE. *(to* **TONI***)* You. Get over here.

TONI. I don't wanna look.

LAURIE. We're all in on this.

MELINDA. Yeah, Toni – you and Hope are accessories, right Tuckett?

TONI. I did not accessorize. I didn't do one thing!

*(***LAURIE*** *glares at* **TONI** *threateningly.* **TONI** *crosses to the trunk.)*

MELINDA. *(to* **TONI***)* Not so pretty now, is she?

TONI. *(reluctantly peeking in)* She looks awful.

HOPE. I can't tell if she's dead or what.

LAURIE. Say somethin', Shanda.

TONI. She's twitching, see?

HOPE. *(distraught)* Why won't she die for Christ sake!

LAURIE. Let's get her out.

TONI. For what?

MELINDA. I'm not touchin' her. Hope, you do it.

HOPE. Ass hole. Why I gotta do it?

LAURIE. Are you my friend? Then prove it. OK, Mel, you get the two-litre. Toni, get back in the car. Hope, help me with Shanda.

*(***TONI*** *returns to the car and turns on the radio: a song like Mariah Carey's "I'll Be There".* * *She bites her hand*

to keep from crying. **HOPE** *and* **LAURIE** *lift* **SHANDA** *out of the trunk as* **MELINDA** *gets a two-litre out of the backseat.* **LAURIE** *and* **HOPE** *carry* **SHANDA** *off, and* **MELINDA** *follows. After a few moments,* **MELINDA**, **LAURIE** *and* **HOPE** *reenter.* **LAURIE'S** *bangs are singed.)*

HOPE. Should we hide her in the woods over there?

LAURIE. No one comes way up here.

HOPE. Just in case.

(**HOPE** *follows* **LAURIE** *into the car.* **MELINDA** *joins them.)*

TONI. *(bites her hand so hard she draws blood)* Ow.

HOPE. *(to* **TONI***)* You're bleedin'.

MELINDA. I am so glad that chick is out of my life. Thee End.

LAURIE. Let's get somethin' to eat.

Scene Twenty-Five
McDonald's

(Muzac plays. **LAURIE,** **HOPE,** **TONI** *and* **MELINDA** *sit at a table.* **LAURIE** *and* **MELINDA** *are eating.* **TONI** *and* **HOPE** *look frightened. A payphone is nearby.)*

LAURIE. Anybody want this Potato Plank?

MELINDA. I love those, but they're so greasy I'd break out like crazy if I ate it. I'd look like that chick at school, whatsherface, with those gigantic zits.

TONI. Vickie Wagers.

MELINDA. She gives me the creeps. When I see her in the cafeteria, I can't even eat.

HOPE. *(scared)* What do we do now?

LAURIE. Nothin'. Act like it never happened.

TONI. Maybe we should call the cops and say someone else did it.

LAURIE. They'll throw us all in jail.

HOPE. Who can we tell?

LAURIE. No one. If everybody keeps their mouth shut we'll be alright.

MELINDA. Tuckett's right. If we stick together, we got nothin' to worry about.

HOPE. What if someone finds her?

LAURIE. No one'll recognize her.

TONI. *(to* **LAURIE***)* What happened to your bangs?

LAURIE. It's the new look. You should try it.

*(***LAURIE** *flicks her lighter near* **TONI***'s hair.)*

TONI. Cut it out! I gotta use the phone.

LAURIE. Who you callin' now?

TONI. Leslie. I gotta see if my mom and dad called.

LAURIE. Keep your mouth shut.

*(***TONI** *crosses to phone and dials.)*

LAURIE. If she talks, we're all screwed.

(LAURIE watches TONI, a distance away, talking on the payphone.)

TONI. Hi, Leslie. Did my mom call? Drivin' around with Hope and Melinda and this other girl, Laurie Tuckett. She's really weird. No, she quit and then she came back and then she quit and – *(fighting back tears)* No, nothin's wrong. Well, somethin' happened, Leslie. No, worse. They killed somebody. I'm not kidding. Shanda, the new girl. She's starin' at me, Leslie, I gotta go. McDonalds. I'll tell you the whole thing later.

(TONI hangs up and returns to the table.)

LAURIE. Who'd you call?

TONI. I told you.

LAURIE. What'd you say?

TONI. Leave me alone. Will you take me home now?

LAURIE. One peep out of you and you're dead meat.

TONI. OK!

MELINDA. Promise?

LAURIE. You too, Hope. Not one word.

HOPE. C'mon, Laurie. You know me better.

LAURIE. I don't know what I know anymore.

(LAURIE looks HOPE in the eye. HOPE looks away.)

MELINDA. *(to LAURIE)* Gimme that Potato Plank. I don't want it to go to waste. *(eats it)* I'm gonna hate myself for this later.

(Everyone looks at MELINDA, making her realize what she just said. Silence.)

Scene Twenty-Six
Bedrooms

*(Three bedrooms are onstage: **TONI**'s, **HOPE**'s, and **LAURIE**'s. The action cuts back and forth between them. **TONI** lies on her bed, wide awake, surrounded by stuffed animals. **HOPE**, fully dressed, sits up on her bed, terrified. **LAURIE** and **MELINDA** are in **LAURIE**'s room. **LAURIE** calmly stares at **MELINDA**, who is nervously picking at her nails.)*

MELINDA. There's a ton of dirt under my nails. This is why I hate nails.

LAURIE. Here.

*(**LAURIE** points the Swiss Army knife at **MELINDA**.)*

MELINDA. Get that thing away from me. Is the blood all out of my hair?

LAURIE. Looks like.

MELINDA. When are we gonna wash out the trunk?

LAURIE. When my mom leaves. Cool it.

MELINDA. Did you throw Shanda's bra on the burnpile too?

LAURIE. I'm gonna keep it – like a relic.

MELINDA. You need help, Tuckett.

LAURIE. Want me to channel her? I can get her to talk to us.

MELINDA. I don't want to talk to her. I want to talk to Mandy.

LAURIE. And say what?

MELINDA. Just her, OK Tuckett? Please?

LAURIE. You can do better than that.

MELINDA. Like who, you? Don't get any big ideas.

LAURIE. *(a beat, then)* Tell her come over here. Alone.

MELINDA. It's Saturday – she's probably out somewhere.

*(**MELINDA** dials, as **LAURIE** begins to channel **SHANDA**. In **HOPE**'s bedroom, **SHANDA**'s watch suddenly begins to play "It's a Small World." **HOPE**, hysterical, searches for the watch, but can't find it anywhere.)*

LAURIE. I feel Shanda's presence. Shanda, are you here? Talk to me, Shanda. Tell me what it's like to be dead.

(HOPE *finds* SHANDA*'s watch in her coat pocket and shuts it off.*)

MELINDA. Her father hates me. I had to beg him to tell me where Mandy was.

LAURIE. Where is she?

MELINDA. At the mall with Fred somethin'.

LAURIE. Who's he?

MELINDA. He's like her fake boyfriend. He has a car. Let's go find her.

LAURIE. Call customer service – they'll page her.

MELINDA. She's gonna be pissed, I know it. (*near tears*) I gotta call Crystal first. C'mon, Tuckett. I've known her since first grade. (*dials*) I'll be quick. Hey, Crystal. You're not gonna believe it. Somethin' terrible happened. We killed Shanda. You know – the little girl. I can't talk –

(LAURIE *grabs the phone from* MELINDA *and slams it down.*)

MELINDA. These are my friends, Tuckett! Just 'cause you ain't got any!

LAURIE. Hope's my friend.

MELINDA. Not anymore.

(HOPE *and* TONI *talk to each other on the phone.*)

HOPE. I'm losin' it, girl. Can you come over?

TONI. D'you try and go to sleep?

HOPE. I'm scared of bein' alone in the dark. I been up for like, 36 hours.

TONI. Me too. And I'm stayin' up. I'm afraid Laurie and Melinda are gonna come and kill me. I almost didn't answer the phone.

HOPE. They're not gonna kill anybody else so soon. Please, Toni? My brothers took the truck to the body shop and I'm here by myself.

TONI. Me too. My mom and dad went to Kroger's. I gotta take a shower first. We goin' out?

HOPE. Wanna?

TONI. What if Laurie and Melinda try to find us?

HOPE. Let's go somewhere they don't go.

TONI. Anderson's maybe?

HOPE. I don't feel like bowlin'.

TONI. Nathan'll be there. He works at the snack bar now.

(**LAURIE** *lies on the floor with her eyes closed.* **MELINDA** *watches the door anxiously.* **AMANDA** *enters.* **MELINDA** *runs to her and hugs her.*)

MELINDA. Baby, I'm so glad you're here. I done somethin' really really bad. Don't hate me, Mandy.

AMANDA. Calm down, Mel.

(**AMANDA** *notices* **LAURIE** *and separates from* **MELINDA.**)

AMANDA. *(to* **LAURIE***)* Hey.

LAURIE. *(gives* **AMANDA** *an evil look)* Hey.

AMANDA. What's goin' on?

MELINDA. We killed Shanda. I just wanted to feel good and beat her up but it went too far.

AMANDA. Yeah, sure.

MELINDA. I'm not kiddin'. I told her if she didn't stay away from you she was dead, didn't I?

AMANDA. No, you said I was dead. Where is she?

MELINDA. On Lemon Road.

AMANDA. Where's that?

MELINDA. See, honey, me and Toni and Hope –

AMANDA. Those guys were with you?

LAURIE. We're all in on it.

MELINDA. We smacked her around and then we didn't know what to do with her so we put her in the trunk and went country cruisin'.

LAURIE. She kept on makin' noise so I smashed her head with the tire iron, like – fifty times.

MELINDA. Don't listen to her, baby. She's just showin' off.

AMANDA. Why didn't you just drop Shanda off somewhere?

MELINDA. She'd tell!

(It's quiet a moment.)

AMANDA. You guys are full of it.

*(**LAURIE** exits.)*

MELINDA. It's all Tuckett's fault, Mandy. She told me in the car it was her destiny to kill somebody – she didn't care who.

AMANDA. *(not convinced)* So what, did she like, drink Shanda's blood?

MELINDA. I don't know, I wasn't with her the whole time. She's mental. Shanda never did a thing to her, but Tuckett wasn't gonna stop 'til –

*(**LAURIE** reenters and waves **SHANDA**'s bloody polka-dot bra in **AMANDA**'s face.)*

LAURIE. Now you believe us?

AMANDA. *(Recognizing the bra, the truth hits her. A beat, then)* Put that away.

LAURIE. Check it out. Her spirit's gonna live in my trunk forever.

AMANDA. Can I get a ride home?

LAURIE. You gonna keep your mouth shut?

MELINDA. Don't talk to Mandy like that! You hear me!? *(to **AMANDA**)* You can't tell anyone, puddin'.

AMANDA. I won't. Just let's go.

MELINDA. Tuckett, I wanna be alone with Mandy for a minute.

LAURIE. *(glares at **MELINDA** and **AMANDA**, then)* One minute. I'll feed the dog.

*(**LAURIE** exits.)*

MELINDA. Get me outta here, Mandy. Let me come home with you!

AMANDA. You know my dad.

MELINDA. *(crying)* I'm sorry, sweetie. I didn't mean to cause all this trouble. You're really gonna miss Shanda, aren't you?

AMANDA. It's OK.

MELINDA. Really?

AMANDA. Forget about it.

MELINDA. I did it out of love for you. I hope you realize that.

AMANDA. I know.

MELINDA. You're not mad at me?

AMANDA. No.

MELINDA. I'm goin' to hell, I know it.

AMANDA. God'll forgive you for anythin' if you're really sorry.

MELINDA. I love you so much, Poo. Do you still love me?

(**AMANDA** *nods.*)

MELINDA. I got my panda ring back. Will you wear it?

(**MELINDA** *puts the ring on* **AMANDA**'s *finger and kisses her.* **LAURIE** *peeks in and watches.*)

AMANDA. What am I gonna do with my shelf?

MELINDA. What shelf?

AMANDA. I made a shelf for Shanda in Wood Shop.

(**TONI** *and* **HOPE** *are together in* **HOPE**'s *bedroom.*)

HOPE. I can't believe you said that! Right at McDonald's with Laurie lookin' at you?

TONI. Leslie knew somethin' was wrong so I just told her.

HOPE. Everythin'?

TONI. Yeah, later on I called her back. She told me to call the cops.

HOPE. That's what Sean said too.

TONI. That kid at Anderson's? You told him!?

HOPE. He could see I was all wigged out.

TONI. You don't even know him! You should've stayed with me and Nathan.

HOPE. D'you tell him too?

TONI. He figured it out.

HOPE. We never shoulda went to Anderson's. I hate bowlin'. I hate those ugly shoes.

TONI. Me too. I can't believe they make you wear them. It's really mean.

(The phone rings. They stop talking and stare at it.)

HOPE. Should I answer it?

TONI. What if it's Laurie and Melinda? What if they saw me come over here? Or this Sean kid, what if he told them what you told him?

HOPE. Blame it on me! Maybe Leslie told them you told her.

TONI. She doesn't even know Laurie.

HOPE. She knows Melinda. And Nathan's Amanda's cousin.

TONI. They're not gonna tell. They're my friends.

HOPE. You were Shanda's friend, right?

(The phone stops ringing. Pause.)

TONI. Hope, were you helpin' Laurie and Melinda outside the Witches' Castle?

HOPE. I was tryin' to pull Shanda away from them.

TONI. Hope, tell me the truth. Were you helpin' them at Lemon Road?

HOPE. *(a beat, then)* Yup.

TONI. How could you do that?

HOPE. Laurie was mad at me for not participatin' more.

TONI. Shanda was still alive!

HOPE. It was all over for her, Toni. There was nothin' we could do.

TONI. I thought you were my friend! I trusted you, and look what you did.

HOPE. I'm sorry.

TONI. You're a murderer!

HOPE. Toni!

TONI. I hate you, Hope. What if I have to go to jail? You screwed up the rest of my life, do you realize that? I'm callin' my mom and dad.

(**TONI** *picks up the phone and dials.*)

Scene Twenty-Seven
Statements

(The scene takes place in various police interview rooms. The girls, in street clothes, address the audience directly.)

VOICE-OVER. The body of a young girl was found on Lemon Road late last night. The victim, Shanda Shanley, was a twelve year-old student at "Our Lady of Perpetual Help." Doctors at King's Daughters Hospital were not immediately able to determine the cause of death. In custody are four juvenile girls ranging in age from 14 to 16. The Judge has ordered that they be held in separate county jails, and not allowed to communicate.

TONI. Melinda and Shanda had got in a lot of fights. See, Melinda is a lesbian and Amanda and Melinda are girlfriend and girlfriend and –

TONI/MELINDA. – Shanda'd been messin' with Amanda –

MELINDA. I just wanted to beat her up – that's it.

TONI. – so Melinda made me call and say Amanda wanted to see her.

HOPE. I went up to Shanda's door with Laurie to get her –

MELINDA. She sat in the front seat –

TONI. Laurie wanted her in the middle so she couldn't jump out I guess.

HOPE. – and I asked her questions that I knew would make Melinda mad.

MELINDA. I put this old, dull knife on her throat. It was nothin', but she got real upset and started cryin' like a little baby.

LAURIE. We went to the Witches' Castle – it's just a place I like, it's not satanic or anythin'. We were all just hangin' out, then Melinda started makin' certain threats.

TONI. They were gonna cut her hair off and I tried to stick up for her.

HOPE. I threatened Shanda with the big knife. And I took her Mickey Mouse watch – Minnie Mouse.

TONI. Melinda wanted to see what Shanda looked like with no clothes then –

LAURIE. All of a sudden Melinda just went off on her. She punched Shanda real hard.

LAURIE/TONI/HOPE. – she started cryin'.

MELINDA. I hit her, no big deal. I had to get it out of my system. Then I'm like, 'Let's take her home now,' but Tuckett pulls me over and goes "She'll tell if we let her go now. We gotta finish her off."

HOPE. I didn't think they were gonna really hurt her.

MELINDA/LAURIE. I don't remember what happened next.

TONI. Shanda ran outside and somewhere in there –

TONI/HOPE. – I tried to help –

HOPE. – Shanda, I mean. Then I just gave up.

LAURIE. There was some rope in my car from when me and my mom brought home the Christmas tree.

LAURIE/MELINDA. Melinda/Tuckett wrapped the rope around Shanda's neck –

MELINDA. – and started pullin' both ends herself. After awhile –

LAURIE/MELINDA. – Shanda quit puttin' up a fight.

MELINDA. – I guess she went unconscious 'cause she stopped kickin'.

MELINDA/HOPE/TONI/LAURIE. They put her in the trunk –

HOPE/TONI. – and we drove to Five Star. I was gonna tell the lady/Nathan what was goin' on – but I didn't.

MELINDA/LAURIE/HOPE/TONI. Shanda starts bangin' –

MELINDA/LAURIE. – so we rode to this little logging road –

LAURIE. – I wanted to be near my house.

TONI. They didn't want her makin' any more noise I guess.

HOPE/TONI. Me and Toni/Me and Hope stayed in the back seat.

HOPE. I had enough by now.

MELINDA. I hate talkin' about this, but –

LAURIE/MELINDA. Melinda/Tuckett put the knife on Shanda's neck –

LAURIE. – and was steppin' on it.

MELINDA. Tuckett wanted me to hold the knife while she tried to kick it in but I wouldn't.

LAURIE. She told me to help her but I said 'no' so she grabs my hand and puts it on top of hers and starts stabbin'. I yanked my hand away –

MELINDA/LAURIE. I was shocked –

MELINDA. – I mean, I was actually like, frozen. Shanda stopped makin' noise.

LAURIE. We finally get to my room but pretty soon –

LAURIE/MELINDA/HOPE. – Shanda started bangin' again –

LAURIE/MELINDA. – and woke up the dog –

TONI. Sparky.

LAURIE. – so I go out to the car and opened the trunk. Shanda was shiverin' and I held her hand and told her not to worry. Then I closed the trunk, not all the way but half way to where it'd stay open. I was hopin' she'd run away.

MELINDA. The bangin' stops and here comes Tuckett back in with this crazy look in her eye.

TONI/HOPE. She wanted to go cruisin' but I didn't want to –

HOPE. – get back in that car – I mean –

HOPE/TONI. – Shanda was still in the trunk.

HOPE. So we took a nap.

LAURIE. It seemed like –

LAURIE/MELINDA. – we were drivin' out there forever –

MELINDA. – it seemed like. Just –

MELINDA/LAURIE. – waitin' for Shanda to die.

MELINDA. – but she wouldn't.

LAURIE/MELINDA. So just kept cruisin' all night long.

HOPE. The sun came up and –

TONI/HOPE. Melinda and Laurie came back –

TONI. – all bloody. Laurie even had blood in her hair.

TONI/HOPE. They said, 'We're gonna put an end to Shanda once and for all – '

TONI. – and I said, 'Take me home right now.'

MELINDA/LAURIE. Lightin' Shanda on fire was Tuckett's/ Melinda's idea.

MELINDA. She said she always wanted to watch somebody burn.

HOPE. The only way we wouldn't get caught was if no one could tell it was Shanda when they found her.

LAURIE. Melinda was the burner. Me and Hope and Toni – we were just scared so we went along for the ride.

TONI. But I didn't go home 'til – after.

HOPE/LAURIE. We went to Clark's Gas Station –

TONI. I was gonna get a can of Diet Pepsi but Melinda goes 'get a two-litre' so I did and we drank some.

HOPE. Laurie poured the rest out and filled it up with gas –

TONI. I thought she just wanted more gas in case she ran out drivin' around.

MELINDA. Hope knew a place we could go –

TONI/HOPE/LAURIE. – so we rode –

TONI. – out past the Chew Mail Pouch Tobacco Barn –

HOPE. – down this gravel road where kids go and get drunk.

LAURIE. When we got to the cornfields, I backed in and parked.

HOPE/TONI. Laurie opened the trunk –

TONI. – and made me look inside. Shanda looked like that girl in the movie "Carrie" when her friends dump blood on her at the prom.

HOPE/LAURIE. We lifted her out and laid her on the ground.

LAURIE. All four of us.

HOPE. Melinda wouldn't touch her. She started the whole thing and now the fucking princess was makin' us finish it.

TONI. I went back in the car and was listenin' to the radio. I didn't really see who did what. Hope poured the gas, supposedly but I'm not sure.

HOPE. Laurie told me to do it, but she didn't make me. I did it all by myself.

MELINDA. Tuckett pulls out her lighter and –

HOPE. Shanda was woked up now.

MELINDA/LAURIE. – she started cryin'.

HOPE. She knew what was gonna happen next.

LAURIE. I didn't light her on fire. Melinda and Hope were standin' right near Shanda and I personally feel that Melinda did it.

MELINDA. Tuckett kneels down and says 'Are you ready to die?'

LAURIE. I knelt down to try to get her to talk to me. All of a sudden –

LAURIE/MELINDA. – the fire went –

LAURIE. – up in my face and singed my bangs.

MELINDA. – like – poof.

TONI. Next thing I know, I smell smoke.

LAURIE/HOPE. I looked in the flames and –

LAURIE/MELINDA. – I saw Shanda's face and –

HOPE. – I felt sick –

MELINDA. – her eyes were rollin' back in her head

MELINDA/LAURIE. – I ran to the car.

TONI. They all piled in and Laurie and –

TONI/LAURIE. – Melinda were/was laughin'.

HOPE. I was in outer space somewhere.

LAURIE/TONI/MELINDA/HOPE. I looked back and –

MELINDA. – it was horrible. Her face was like, melting.

LAURIE. – she was tryin' to stand up.

TONI. – I said, "Goodbye, Shanda."

HOPE. – that was the last time I saw her. That's how I always see her now.

HOPE/TONI/MELINDA/LAURIE. Then we went to McDonalds.

Scene Twenty-Eight

(**AMANDA** *is alone in her room. Music: a song like Wilson Phillip's "Release Me".**)

AMANDA. *(reading notes)* "Dear Amanda. My name is Shanda with a "d." It rhymes with yours. Why don't you call me sometime? *(another note)* I loved last night. I want it again and again. *(another note)* I know you told me not to worry, but I'm afraid somethin' really bad's gonna happen. *(another note)* Mandy, I miss the touch of your soft body. Always and forever. Love, Shanda." *(***AMANDA*** breaks down.)*

Scene Twenty-Nine
Psychologists

(The scene takes place in various psychologists' rooms over a period of time.)

MELINDA. I loved Daddy to death. I'd do anything for him. We had secret places where me and him would go. He liked to tickle my feet or he'd lay me out on the picnic table and pop my pimples.

HOPE. I played flute in the school band when I was little. I was pretty good. Now I'm into more hard-core kinda music.

LAURIE. The worst thing that ever happened to me was bein' born. All my memories are pitch black.

MELINDA. Daddy was a real gentleman. He taught me how a man is supposed to treat a lady, like you should pull the chair out and set the woman down and push it in and be like, really sweet.

TONI. Everyone thinks I got my mom and dad wrapped around my little finger. It's true, I guess. They buy me all kinds of stuff, and I never had to do any chores or anything.

HOPE. My house is real rowdy. Ev'ry time my mom and dad get drunk, they end up in a big brawl. My brothers, too – they're always beatin' the shit out of each other. It's kinda cool.

MELINDA. He was never nice to my mom. He'd like, poke her and goose her. He got off on the strangest things, like when you had to go to the bathroom, he'd make you pee in a little Dixie cup and he'd watch to see how much you could get in.

LAURIE. I got a beatin' every day because I wouldn't go to church. My mom only stopped because the welfare worker started comin' around. That's when I started to quote 'worship the devil' and wear black. But I was never really into Satan. I just acted evil to piss her off – and scare the Preps.

TONI. Kids at school thought I was a Prep 'cause of my clothes, but I didn't really fit in with those guys. I didn't fit in with the Alternatives neither. I don't really care about fittin' in – I just wish I was prettier and more popular – like Melinda.

HOPE. I felt bad for Laurie 'cause no one wanted to hang around with her. Kids at school'd make fun of her 'cause she was always like, in and outta mental hospitals. Her mom was intense.

LAURIE. She said I was evil, and I was gonna burn in eternal flames if I didn't receive the Holy Ghost. I had a three-foot doll named Patty. My mom thought she had strange eyes so she put her in the furnace and made me watch her burn.

TONI. I believe in God and premarital sex. I don't believe in abortion or anythin' that can kill someone. And I believe in havin' babies out of wedlock. Nathan and I are goin' steady again but it's hard 'cause I'm in jail.

HOPE. I never had no real boyfriend, but I had sex a lot.

MELINDA. Daddy slept in my room off and on – right up 'til the day he left. He'd say, 'Lindystar, let's go to bed' and he'd carry me upstairs.

LAURIE. Everytime I got raped, I'd black out, and when I woke up, I'd have this new person livin' inside me. First there was Sissy – she's a brat. Then Sara – she's left-handed. Then last year, Deanna the Vampire.

MELINDA. I'm not gonna testify against him. He didn't molest me – we was just really close.

TONI. My philosophy on life is it could be a lot better. I mean, I watched Shanda get killed. But I guess it could be worse. I could've been the one that got murdered.

LAURIE. Look, how does this work? Say Deanna was present at the time of the murder – you can't punish her without punishin' Sissy and Sara who weren't even there.

MELINDA. He smacked my mom around a lot and one time, he threw her out of the car – then he drove Florida and never came back.

HOPE. Laurie told me to pour the gas and friends are supposed to help each other is how I see it. And I wanted to get the whole thing over with.

MELINDA. He sends me this picture, and on the back it says, 'Here's your new step-mom.' I stayed in my room cryin' for like, months after that. I tried to slash my wrists. My skin was breakin' out all over.

LAURIE. Sure I like to put people on, but my personalities or spirits or whatever you call 'em are not fake. They're real to me. I need them. I don't have any friends, and my mom hasn't visited me once since I been in jail.

TONI. 'Wish' by Toni Lynn Lincoln. I wish I could erase that night, then everything would be alright. But I know I shan't, for the simple fact I can't. I hope that God forgives me, so I won't drown in that fiery sea. I wish I could go home, and hide away like a little gnome.

MELINDA. I went out with some guys, but they was all pigs so I thought I'd give girls a try. I met Mandy and we hit it off real good. She even looked like my Dad. When the kids at Hazelwood called us dykes, Mandy'd let 'em have it. But she had a rovin' eye – and there was this new girl – Shanda.

HOPE. What I learned from this experience is don't just go along with people you know are doin' wrong and not to, you know, crack under peer pressure and to basically be my own person which I didn't do.

TONI. I didn't do anything wrong. I was just in the wrong place at the wrong time. I would like to testify against the other girls so Shanda can rest in peace, and I can get out on bail.

LAURIE. I need help. If you guys keep me in jail, I'll kill myself – or kill someone else.

MELINDA. As soon as I seen the way Mandy looked at her, I knew there was gonna be trouble.

(As their sentences are announced, each girl stands and poses for a mugshot.)

VOICE-OVER. Mary Laurine Tuckett: Sixty years – thirty with good behavior. Melinda Dufay: Sixty years – thirty with good behavior. Hope Richey: Fifty years – twenty-five with good behavior. Toni Lynn Lincoln: Twenty years – ten with good behavior. After over a year in separate county jails, all four girls have been remanded to Indiana Women's Prison.

(A jail door slams.)

Scene Thirty
Hope's Cell at Indiana Women's Prison

HOPE. Dear Mrs. Shanley. I know that you can never forgive me but I would like to say some things to you. I feel so much sadness for your little girl. She was too young to die – she had her whole life ahead of her. What we did was cold-hearted and disgusting. You have the right to hate me. I wish there was somethin' I could do for you but I know there isn't. I just wanted to tell you how sorry I am. Yours truly, Hope Richey.

Scene Thirty-One
Visiting Room at Indiana Women's Prison

(A pane of glass separates the two girls. A bell rings.)

MELINDA. We got about one minute left. This guard's a bitch.

AMANDA. I like her moustache.

MELINDA. I hate it in this big jail, honey. These uniforms are so ugly. I can't go to the bathroom because I have to pull it all the way down and the men guards see me. And the food is awful.

AMANDA. I brought you a burger, but they wouldn't let me bring it in.

MELINDA. I hate it when you leave, Poo. I'm so lonesome in here it's like I'm goin' nuts.

AMANDA. You'll get used to it.

MELINDA. My dad got arrested for molestation 'cause of what they made me say on the stand. I am so pissed and hurt.

AMANDA. What about your mom?

MELINDA. She calls me every day and we both bawl our eyes out. I keep readin' your old letters over and over, baby.

AMANDA. Want me to bring you some magazines?

MELINDA. I mean you ain't wrote me nothin' in a while.

AMANDA. I been workin' lots of hours.

MELINDA. Tell me the truth, Mandy. You seein' someone else?

AMANDA. Yeah.

MELINDA. Do I know her?

AMANDA. No. This girl Francine. She works with me at Arby's.

MELINDA. Do you love her?

AMANDA. I guess.

MELINDA. *(crushed)* Well, you know what they say – if you love somethin', let it go and if it comes back then it was meant to be. Know what I mean?

AMANDA. *(not sure)* I guess.

MELINDA. I can't stand this glass.

AMANDA. It's like a drive-through window.

MELINDA. Like I'm workin' and you're drivin' through. *(a beat, then)* Listen, OK, honey? Go ahead, play around and have fun –

AMANDA. You play around too.

MELINDA. OK. But remember, when I get out, you belong to me, OK?

AMANDA. I'll be, um – seventy-six years old.

MELINDA. With good time credit, I could be forty-six when I get out.

AMANDA. OK.

MELINDA. I really messed up, Mandy.

(They touch the glass.)

I wanna hold you so bad.

(They kiss the glass.)

You are so damn cute.

AMANDA. Bye, Mel.

MELINDA. Always and forever – don't forget!

Scene Thirty-Two
Dining Room At The Indiana Womens Prison

*(One year later. **MELINDA** sits at a table eating. An empty table is nearby.)*

VOICE-OVER. Ladies, today is the last day for you to turn in your requests for visitation hours. Remember, Indiana Women's Prison does not accept late requests. Tonight's movie is *Ghost*, a supernatural thriller with Whoopi Goldberg and Patrick Swayze, in the Southeast Wing at 6 p.m.

*(**LAURIE** approaches with a tray, and sits next to **MELINDA**.)*

MELINDA. Where you been, Tuckett?

LAURIE. Isolation.

MELINDA. What'd you do?

LAURIE. I yanked a sink out of the wall.

MELINDA. Already? You just got here.

LAURIE. They put me on sanitation – cleanin' toilets and shit. I said, "Fuck this."

MELINDA. You're not gonna earn any good time credit. You'll be in here till you rot, and make Shanda's mom happy.

LAURIE. I like isolation. I go into another realm when I'm in there.

MELINDA. You're fucked up. Look, there's Carrissa – the one who gave me these hickeys. *(showing off her hickeys)*

LAURIE. What's she in for?

MELINDA. She killed her kids – and now she's pregnant. The chicks in this place are crazy.

LAURIE. It's like the big city in here compared to county jail.

MELINDA. *(pulling her uniform down in the front)* And look – I got this big one from a male guard.

LAURIE. You screwed a guy?

MELINDA. I didn't have to. He said if I flashed him, he'd give me cigarettes and gum. So we went to a security pod. These other girls think he's hot and I wanted to throw it in their face.

LAURIE. *(showing razor)* Look what I got. *(She shows* **MELINDA** *a razor blade hidden in a handkerchief.)* I'll take care of anyone who gives you a hard time.

MELINDA. You still love my ass, don't you Tuckett?

LAURIE. Whatever.

MELINDA. You don't need a razor to show these girls who's boss. They saw us on TV – they're scared of us. I already sold my autograph for five bucks. Look, here comes Hope. Hey, girl!

(**HOPE** *enters with a tray, walks by* **LAURIE** *and* **MELINDA** *and sits at the empty table.)*

LAURIE. Sit with us, Hope.

MELINDA. Yeah, we ain't seen you in a whole year. Let's catch up.

LAURIE. You don't wanna be our friend no more?

HOPE. Not really.

MELINDA. What were you doin' in the library, Hope?

HOPE. I seen the two of you staring at me. Ain't you got nothin' better to do?

MELINDA. You a Prep now?

HOPE. This ain't Junior High.

MELINDA. The cafeteria tables look the same.

HOPE. Don't bother me, okay?

LAURIE. *(sincerely)* I'll always be your friend, Hope. Whether you want me to or not.

(**TONI** *enters with a tray. She sees* **HOPE** *and approaches, then notices* **LAURIE** *and* **MELINDA**, *and hesitates.)*

MELINDA. Where's your little friend Toni? D'she get transferred yet?

HOPE. Last week. The day after we got sentenced.

LAURIE. *(pleased)* She thought she'd get off if she turned state's evidence – but the judge hated her.

MELINDA. Where's she been hidin'?

HOPE. She's up in line gettin' food.

MELINDA. *(spotting* **TONI***)* Toni-Roni!

HOPE. Sit down, Toni.

MELINDA. We won't bite.

LAURIE. I might.

> *(Reluctantly,* **TONI** *sits next to Hope.)*

MELINDA. Here we are, girls – the four of us, back together at last, just like the old days!

HOPE. *(to* **TONI***)* You alright? You look all white.

TONI. My neck hurts but I'm OK.

HOPE. What happened?

TONI. *(a beat then, simply, to* **HOPE***)* I tried to hang myself.

HOPE. Why'd you do somethin' stupid like that?

TONI. I don't want to be here.

MELINDA. So you strung yourself up?

TONI. What do you care?

LAURIE. How come you're not dead?

HOPE. *(to* **LAURIE***)* That's enough.

> *(***LAURIE*** moves in next to* **TONI***.)*

LAURIE. *(to* **TONI***, threateningly)* You're a traitor. Know what happens to traitors?

TONI. You're a murderer.

LAURIE. That's right.

> *(***LAURIE*** pins* **TONI***'s arm to the table, takes out the razor and holds it over* **TONI***'s wrist.)*

TONI. Quit it!

HOPE. *(to* **LAURIE***)* Stop it. Now. You hear me?

> *(***HOPE*** stares* **LAURIE*** down.* **LAURIE*** releases* **TONI***, who is trembling, and moves away.* **MELINDA*** moves to* **TONI***'s table.)*

MELINDA. Toni, I'll make Tuckett leave you alone for ten bucks a week.

TONI. OK.

HOPE. Don't say yeah so quick. Where you gonna get the money?

TONI. My allowance.

LAURIE. Mel, the monitor's eyeballin' us. Let's beat it.

MELINDA. Bye bye, girls.

LAURIE. *(to* **TONI***)* You're not gettin' out of this place alive.

(**MELINDA** *and* **LAURIE** *walk off.*)

TONI. I'm glad I told the cops. I don't belong here. I didn't do anything.

HOPE. That's right, you didn't do anything. You shoulda done somethin'. We both shoulda.

TONI. I hugged Shanda and told her I was sorry!

HOPE. You got a lot to learn, Toni. I can help you. I been takin' classes. I wanna get some psychology degrees and be a child psychologist. I think I have a lot to offer other kids after what we been through.

TONI. You hated school, Hope. You never did homework.

HOPE. At county jail, I made friends with the older girls. I liked the way they weren't so worried about what everybody else was thinkin' like us young girls.

TONI. My mom and dad said if I just told the judge what happened, I wouldn't go to jail. I hate jail! I can't take it.

HOPE. We'll figure something out. Just don't do anything stupid.

TONI. What if Laurie really tries to kill me?

HOPE. She's just acting tough. I can see right through her now.

TONI. *(a beat, then)* She killed Shanda, didn't she?

(**TONI** *looks* **HOPE** *in the eye.* **SHANDA** *enters.*)

HOPE. Don't worry 'bout her. I got your back.

(**HOPE** *walks off.* **TONI** *sits alone, frightened.*)

SHANDA. Well, this year, I'm goin' to a different school – Hazelwood Jr. High. Thank God! I was so sick of St. Paul's. Now I get to wear cool clothes – if my mom lets me. I wish my mom would understand that I don't want to be 12. I want to be 13. I want to talk on the phone on school nights and have people sleep over. I don't know anybody at Hazelwood. I'm sort of scared I won't fit in. I hope they like me. Love, Shanda.

The End

Also by
Rob Urbinati...

West Moon Street

Please visit our website **samuelfrench.com** for complete
descriptions and licensing information.

From the Reviews of
HAZELWOOD JR. HIGH...

"In this fierce, disturbing lament for the death of childhood, the characters
hardly change - but the audience does. Six junior high school kids remain,
through terrible events, suspended in a moral vacuum. We, however, move
from open laughter to uncomfortable giggling to deep, dark silence. Though
the play retains a deadpan documentary feel, withholding judgments and
explanations until near the end, it is very much a dramatic artifice. Urbinati
immerses us in the girls' world. He sweeps us into the warped logic by which
a lunchroom tiff escalates into a dreadful crime, and this logic is stitched
into dialogue where perspective and proportion are scarily absent. Urbinati
creates a mental jungle in which vampires and cuddly toys, Pentecostal visions
and Kmart are tangled together. Slowly, these juxtapositions lose their humor
and become an angry, insistent protest at the failure of the adult world
to provide these kids with a way through. This is deft and morally serious
writing, never exploitative and ultimately full of pity. Everywhere, there is the
kind of precision and care that such a subject demands."
- Fintan O'Toole, *New York Daily News*

"*Hazelwood Jr. High* is a blistering piece of drama that's conceived and
presented in cinematic terms. Its multiple scenes and locations flow
into each other without a break, building a considerable I can't believe
I'm watching this steam as Urbinati's story veers from puppydog lesbian
romance toward brutal slaughter. The horror of it all is seriocomically
underscored by the typical banalities of teen existence while songs by
Mariah Carey and 1990's girl groups pulse through the air. If you go, better
hang on tight – it's a wicked midnight ride with the rising generation, and
definitely not a show for the squeamish."
- Michael Sommers, *New Jersey Star Ledger*

"Mr. Urbinati has written this in a combination of documentary and
dramatic style, effectively capturing the banality, the provincialism and the
simple mindedness of the girls and their cruelty. While he makes some
gestures in the direction of psychological explanation, the overall effect
– undoubtedly intentional – is the frightful ordinariness of these teenagers.
Even as they stumble toward savagery, they play their boom boxes, eat at
McDonald's, hang out at the mall and gossip about social life."
- Martin Gottfried, *New York Law Journal*

CPSIA information can be obtained
at www.ICGtesting.com
Printed in the USA
BVOW04s1749211216

471464BV00016B/317/P